This is

Zac.

This is

Zeb.

They are very best friends.

They are good at painting and sticking,

dancing round and round, cheering each other up

and having proper adventures.

That is a good kind of best friend to have.

For Kate and Stephanie
(for your faith in
Zac and **Zeb**,
and in me) xxx

First published 2012 by Nosy Crow Ltd
The Crow's Nest, 10a Lant Street
London SE1 1QR
www.nosycrow.com

ISBN 978 0 85763 085 8 (HB)
ISBN 978 0 85763 091 9 (PB)

Nosy Crow and associated logos are trademarks and /or registered
trademarks of Nosy Crow Ltd.

Text copyright © Nosy Crow Ltd 2012
Character and illustrations copyright © Sarah Massini 2012

The right of Sarah Massini to be identified as the illustrator of this work
has been asserted.

A CIP catalogue record for this book is available
from the British Library.

Printed in China

1 3 5 7 9 8 6 4 2

Sarah Massini

Zac and Zeb

and the
Make-Believe
Birthday
Party

nosy
crow

It was **Zac's** birthday.

Birthdays made **Zac** hum with happiness because . . . . . they meant parties . . . .

... friends, yummy food, presents and things that go ...

... pop!

At the end
of his party,

Zac was

still happy . . .

. . . but
Zeb

was glum.

"I want a birthday," glummed **Zeb.**

"You will have
a birthday, Zeb," sang **Zac**.

"Everyone has one.

And guess what?

Your birthday is next!"

Zeb skipped home and thought about his birthday being **next**.

"**Next** means the **next day**. And the **next day** means **tomorrow**," **Zeb** said to himself. "So, **tomorrow** will be **my** birthday party and **my** turn for friends, yummy food, presents and things that go . . . pop!"

When tomorrow
came, it looked a good
day to have a birthday party.

So **Zeb** practised happy humming in different ways and waited for his friends to come and the fun to start.

But no friends came.

No fun started.

Zeb felt glum.

Ratt-a-tatt-tatt!
came a knock on the door.

It was **Zac,** but he was
all by himself.

"Where is everyone?"
said **Zeb.**
"Where's my
birthday party?"

"Your birthday party?"
asked **Zac.**

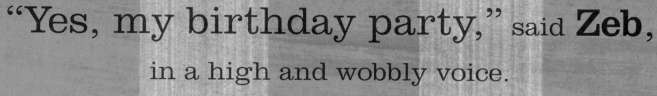

"Yes, my birthday party," said **Zeb**,
in a high and wobbly voice.

"You said my birthday was next,
and now it's here."

"Whoops," said Zac.

"I've got an idea," **Zac** added quickly.

"Wait here!"

Soon **Zac** was back.

"Let's **pretend** it's your birthday!" he said.

"But I haven't got a present," wobbled **Zeb.**

"We'll make one!" said **Zac.**

"What would you like?" **Zeb** thought.

"A space rocket!" he shouted.

"Let's make a space rocket!"

So the two friends got to work and made a
supercharged space rocket
and painted their very own flag.

Then they put on their helmets, pulled down their goggles and . . .

5, 4, 3, 2, 1

-blast off!-

away they zoomed,
on a make-believe birthday
adventure!

They looped the loop through stars that sparkled.

They dodged space-rocks

that looked like yellow balloons ready to go . . . pop!

Then they touched down their . . . . . . supercharged space rocket . . . .

. . . on the **moon.**

They planted their flag,
and had a yummy birthday picnic.

"Thank you, Zac," said Zeb. "It's been the best make-believe birthday ever!"

"And do you know what makes it even better?" asked Zac, as they climbed back into their space rocket . . .

. . . and flew home in time for bed . . . .

"I know! I know!"
sang **Zeb.**
"It's my real birthday next!"